A Prayer In Spring

A Prayer In Spring

ROBERT FROST

GRANDMA MOSES

UNIVERSE

This edition published in the United States of America in 2011 by
Universe Publishing
A Division of Rizzoli International Publications, Inc.
300 Park Avenue South
New York, NY 10010
www.rizzoliusa.com

2011 2012 2013 2014 / 10 9 8 7 6 5 4 3 2 1

Printed in China

ISBN: 978-0-7893-2226-5

Library of Congress Control Number: 2010934737

For further information on Grandma Moses, please visit www.grandmamoses.com and www.gseart.com

Oh, give us pleasure in the flowers to-day;
And give us not to think so far away

As the uncertain harvest; keep us here
All simply in the springing of the year.

Oh, give us pleasure in the orchard white,
Like nothing else by day, like ghosts by night;

And make us happy in the happy bees,
The swarm dilating round the perfect trees.

And make us happy in the darting bird
That suddenly above the bees is heard,

The meteor that thrusts in with needle bill,
And off a blossom in mid air stands still.

For this is love and nothing else is love,
The which it is reserved for God above

To sanctify to what far ends He will,
But which it only needs that we fulfil.

Grandma Moses (1860-1961) is one of the most important self-taught artists of the 20th century. Born Anna Mary Robertson, she achieved a celebrity that transcended the normal boundaries of the folk art movement. Grandma Moses invented a unique style that proved enormously popular, and its influence may be seen to this day.

Robert Frost (1874-1963) is perhaps one of the most quoted and celebrated of American poets. Born in California, he is most associated with New England, where he lived, taught, and wrote for almost fifty years. A four-time winner of the Pulitzer Prize for Poetry, his influence over contemporary literature is incalculable.